Group Hug

Written by

JEAN REIDY

Illustrated by

JOEY CHOU

There once was a slug,
needing someone to hug.

SHRUG.

Along came a beetle,
a lonely ol' bug.

"You need a hug?
I have one," said Slug,
"to keep your heart snug!"

HUG!

Nearby was Mouse
with a case of the grumps.

She'd hit a few bumps,
and was down in the dumps.

"Chin up," said Bug.
"There's no need to stew.
We'll help you pull through.
Your hug's overdue!"

GROUP HUG!

Then up shuffled Skunk,
lost control of his smell.
And Squirrel, as well,
had been sprayed. You could tell!
Their fragrance so foul,
proved hard to undo.
"Never mind the slight pong,"
said Mouse. "Come, join our throng!"

GROUP HUG!

Now Beaver was busy,
too busy for friends.
When building his dam,
his job never ends.

"Take five! A quick break!"
said Squirrel — Skunk too —
"Please join our crew.
Let the hugging ensue!"

GROUP HUG!

Along plodded Porcupine,
feeling quite prickly.
I didn't say sickly,
just ploddy and prickly.

She needed a hug,

'cause hugs had been lacking.

Said Beaver, "Dear Porcupine —

send those quills packing!"

SHAKE!
SHAKE!
SHAKE!

GROUP HUG!

A groundhog,
forgotten.

A goose, out of luck.

A fox,

labelled "Sneaky".

A moose, feeling stuck.

The group hug stretched wide
and the group hug stretched tall,

making plenty of room
for those antlers and all.

Then . . .

along lumbered Bear
needing someone to care.
(Not to snack on, I swear . . .)
Yet they shouted,
"BEWARE!"

And off scampered Squirrel
and Skunk and the smell.
Off scooted Fox and Groundhog as well.
Off scurried Porcupine, no longer prickly.
Goose and Moose, also,
skedaddled quite quickly.
Off skittered Mouse,
who was no longer blue.
And Beaver and Bug?
Bear scared them off too!

Till the only ones left
were brave Slug, and Bear.

And Slug said, "Hey, Bear!
I have more hugs to share!"

You see, Slug knew a secret,
as sure as she'd shrugged —
— that the hugger finds **HAPPY**
As much as the hugged!

HEART TUG!

GROUP HUG!

To Charlie, with oodles of hugs! —J. R.

For Lemon and Kermit, thanks for all the hugs when I needed them —J. C.

First published in Great Britain in 2021 by Scallywag Press Ltd,
10 Sutherland Row, London SW1V 4JT

Originally published in the USA in 2021 by Godwin Books, an imprint of Henry Holt and Company
Henry Holt® is a registered trademark of Macmillan Publishing Group, LLC

Printed on FSC paper in China by Toppan Leefung

001

British Library Cataloguing in Publication Data available

ISBN 978-1-912650-84-2